CW00840246

Introduction.

Thanks for buying this little book. It contains some poems, snippets and songs written in 2019/20. They cover a lot of subjects, mostly daft, but I hope there are a few jewels scattered in with the silly stuff. Dedicated to my brother Tony Berry. He liked some of my stuff and if he liked it that is good enough for me.

Jim Berry 1st September 2020 France.

1.

Do you ever pick your nose when no-ones looking.

Do you ever count your teeth with your tongue.

Do you ever lick the spoon when you are cooking.

Or say you're right when you know that you are wrong.

Have you ever wiped your bum on a dock leaf.

Have you ever had a wee behind a bush.

Have you ever squeezed a spot in the mirror.

Or left front door wide open in a rush.

Have you left your DNA at a crime scene.

Broken out of a high security jail.

Smuggled Kalashnikov rifles out of Russia.

Committed GBH and arson whilst on bail.

Have you ever been a hit man for the Mafia.

Been head of a crime mob in th'East End.

Have you ever told a white lie to your mother.

Not me! I'm just asking for a friend.

2.

I long to be where the streets are quietly lit

Where a far off dog barks at sunset

And the evening cats just sit

On windowsills and walls

Where the river curves tree guarded

Before the crumbling limestone bridge

And the howling moon in silence

Floats above the flint rock ridge

Where the pub lights filter out across the drowsy angled streets

No sound of evening news

No thumping big bass beats

No folded tempting newspapers

No WiFi Internet

No gangs of left and right playing moral roulette

When mans persuasive words have no dominion

A town called No Opinion.

3.

As the barren moon surfed ripples on the waters of Top Lock
Ghosts and angels dusted soot from off their wings.
The great stone flags matt polished by a million trudging feet
The poverty of antlife feeding kings.
No flowers, not a flower, grow between the cracks and edges,
No polished brass, blue plaques, no recognition.
Blood and broken bones, disease and ruined lives,
Fund the grotesque bulging banks, no guilt admission.
Victorian solid monoliths, a testament to power,
Still exist, the gravestones of misdeeds.
Built from cotton, built from coal, built from muscle heart and soul
Built from broken lives left scattered in the weeds.

4.

Anonymity under 7 mile clouds.
We were fishing in the Figure Eight, me and Peter Clare.
When darkness fell mid-morning and silence gulped the air.
Two swans dropped, confused and lost and settled near the reeds.
 The blackest clouds imaginable, fish rushed into the weeds.
The rain a hissing torrent boiled like water in a pan.
A biblical derangement turned to madness in the land.
That day from the Atlantic storm clouds seven miles deep.
Advanced across the Lancashire Plain and pulverized the sheep.
Sodden walking later talking about clouds seven miles thick!
The immensity amazed me as I did the arithmetic.
I said "I'll put this in a poem one day just you wait and see!"

Peter said "Exaggerate as usual but don't bloody mention me!"

(Peter Clare is a great friend and his dad was mayor of Howfen and a great Lancashire poet by the way it is true about the seven miles thick clouds)

5.

Do you not know who I am?

Do you not know who I am! I am an MP and a Lord.

What's wrong with smacking ladies bottoms?

Don't be so absurd.

She was a commoner for god's sake,

Serving me a bloody drink.

She wanted her bottom slapping, they all do doncha think.

How bloody lucky she was, meeting a man like me

With a shooting lodge in Scotland and a mansion by the sea.

I was in a bloody good mood and I like a laugh and a sup

Oh give her a few tenners, shut the silly woman up.

This is a private club! Who's that rough looking man?

Her brother wants to smack me too? Do you not know who I am!!

6.

It started with her lapping shandy from an ashtray in't beer garden.

Now her mood swings have become hyperbolic.

I'm worried about her health, will her arteries start to harden?

I fear my little dog's an alcoholic.

She started off on bitter but soon moved onto stronger things

I was hoping that her habit wasn't chronic

Till I found her in the kitchen with that cat from across the road

Eating Tasty Treats and drinking gin and tonic.

She'll start a fight for nothing, her tempers always frayed.

Especially when she's nursing an hangover.

Plus the company she's keeping and the hours that she's sleeping

And barking along to the tune of the Wild Rover.

But I can't watch this and keep quiet I have put her on a diet.

Less red meat, more green beans and a carrot.

She reluctantly agreed, to wash it down though said she'd need

Aperitifs and a well decanted claret.

I think I've got the problem solved, I need to get involved

She needs exercise and trained like an Alsatian

But when we go out on a walk she doesn't have to talk

She just drags me in't Red Lion for the duration.

7

So I'm sittin' here in't chair, it's a frantic world out there.

And I'm grateful I've got shelter, I've got food.

Few problems in't grand scheme,

Apart from't brain and fiendish dreams,

Nowt wrong for me a bit of solitude.

I feel God's love in the trees, from the west a cooling breeze.

Little dog'll bring her ball and I'll throw it.

Not much like the Dalai Lama but I don't need human drama.

I'm lucky to be me and I know it.

But men are funny creatures unknow the wisdom of life's teachers

Find trouble and ordeals in empty spaces.

Turn to mischief, turn to sin, give up quiet for hellish din.

Then yearn for love and peace that that replaces.

8.

I was old enough to join the army and too young to buy a pint.

I was thinking that the third world war was due.

From 1918 to 1939 only 21 short years

And from 45 to now was 22.

So I walked down't fields and fished in bomb holes

For shimmering crucian carp

And I wondered then if I could fight like they did

With mi head blown off and me spirit gone

Up in heaven playin' th'Harp.

There were Viet Nam and Bob's Hard Rain

I put a maggot on the hook.

Can't pick up the fear and panic

of a young soldier from a book.

So I selfishly tried to forget the horror of those young men.

Checked me float and checked me bait and cast out in't pond again.

Wingates were beckoning and underage or not

Them first few pints of bitter undid that sickly knot.

9.

Country Dance

My woman she is mad at me,

She says I don't pay her no attention.

But I like fishin', beer and guns,

And other things I shouldn't mention.

"If you don't change I'm gonna find,

Someone who appreciates my body and my mind"

She says "I'll give you one more chance,

Take me to the country dance"

Yes I'll take you dearest pal

I'll learn the steps and we'll do great.

You are such a dainty gal

And I throw javelin for the state.

You say if I don't change you'll find,

Someone who appreciates your body and your mind.

But I've been told she's seeing Frank.

That loser who works at the bank.

Stamp your feet and dosey doh.

Grab your girl and away we go.

Spin her round and let her go.

Where she crashes no-one knows,

She says that she's gonna find,

Someone appreciates her body and her mind.

Pick her up by the heel and toe.

Out the window. There she goes!

10.

Pie Ella from Wigan.

There's a Spanish wench in Wigan called Pie Ella.

She were looking for a full time fancy fella.

I took her for some tapas and pork scratchings

All the time romantic plans we were hatching.

(chorus)

Oohh Pie Ella I'm your fella,

After fourteen pints of Stella,

Let me share your umberella as we walk through Whelley in the rain.

I went round to hers to get a cup of sugar

She says Buenos Nochas you sexy little bugger

Can you lend me one of your tobaccas

If you do I'll let you play with my maracas.

As we walk through Whelley in the rain.

One night were supping pints of tango.

She gets up on't table doing a fandango.

I said "Get down, we can't have senoritas"

"Showing off their bits to all these old pie eaters".

Then in Ince we'd been on an all nighter.

She said I fancy you Amor as a bullfighter

She said I can see you in tight pants upon the cinders

I said I think I'll stick to cleaning people's windows.

But now that I am overweight and boozy

I can't keep up with my european floozy

She's turned a bit vivacious and outlandish

And she's left me for a plumber's mate from Standish.

11.

Jim Berry's 2030 Dream.

I bought a disposable moped and I rode to another town.

I threw it in the recycling then I went to look around.

Registered my gender at the post office, have to do that every day.

I said "I'm still the same" she said "You have to do it anyway"

50 C in the shade I was glad I'd brought my flask.

When a man said I don't recognise you, please put on your mask.

Antifa and BLM had occupied the town hall.

They said "Pay your fee or take the knee, it's really now your call"

I said "I'm not a racist!" they said "That's just not enough"

"Either pay your fee or take the knee or we're going to get tough"

Being short of cash and courage, removed my principles like a hat.

I took the knee, they set me free and that was that.

I got some Covid 30 pills from a robot in the kiosk.

Then got my "I love Mecca" card stamped at the mosque.

I tried to make some friends but I ended up in jail.

The charge? You're a privileged white heterosexual old male.

I said "I'm open minded" I'm just trying to keep things sweet.

They took both my George Orwell books and threw me in the street.

I went to find the airport but they'd fixed the gates with glue.

They said we're still negotiating things with the EU.

I stood out in the street screaming "I am just a man"

When a gang of crazed transexuals ran over me in their van.

I was stood on Blackpool tower and I was threatening to jump.

There was another bloke beside me and he looked like Donald Trump.

12.

He were the hardest bastard in Hardtown.

His knuckles were covered in scars.

He were six foot tall and three foot wide.

He was feared in the pubs and the bars.

He'd perfected the swift crunching head butt,

Preceded by a smile and a wink.

Regarded his dropped adversary,

Before continuing to drink his drink.

And he never picked on anyone,

But when violence came his way

Woe betide the perpetrators,

He could always ruin their day.

Then one thing changed his demeanor,

Mildred a frail little lost kitten.

She meowed in his yard one night in the rain.

When he picked her up he were smitten.

He doesn't punch people much these days.

Mildred often gives his finger a chew.

He has to be careful with Mildred.

She's a hard little bastard too!

13.

I could not afford Blonde on Blonde.

When Howfen were just streets

And I knew most folks I'd meet

And going in the library was somehow a posh retreat

Hot Vimto in Tommy Ramsden's

Down the fields the frond on pond

And I could not afford Blonde on Blonde.

Beatles on Luxembourg, Rolling Stones and Kinks

Fishing near the Boneworks

With it's fine eye watering stinks

The A6 shook with lorries

Wingates Square I grew so fond

And I could not afford Blonde on Blonde.

Walking home up Church street in the winter in the dark

Sitting on the cold stone side of Diddy Bottle Park

Wigglesworths was pumping pills

Thornleigh mornings I'd abscond

And I could not afford Blonde on Blonde.

Drink from't taps in New park toilets.

Rationed Polos, getting bored

Tinniswoods side window another thing I couldn't afford

In my rags to meet my girlfriend

Thought I looked like James Bond

And I could not afford Blonde on Blonde.

14.

In the swarming supermarket it was there.

In the silence of my evening it was there.

Not in person, not in meat,

Not in legions of the street.

Not in touching as I climbed the lonely stair, but it was there.

In an unexpected moment it says Hi.

Remember me? I thought I'd said the last goodbye.

Could be a bark, a faint smoke smell,

Reversing car, a far church bell.

I thought that ample time had passed me by, it just says Hi.

When i thought it was dim distant it was here.

So far away I had forgotten, oh so near.

Seeming speeding down the road

A busy mind in overload

Didn't know I was still stuck in second gear, it was just here.

In the back streets of my mind it still survives.

Are there people living warm unhaunted lives.

I keep thinking I am free, that it exists surprises me,

I thought I'd killed it with a million mental knives.

In death it writhes.

15.

You don't have to worry about that today.

Forget it, protect your little self.

Nobody is really that important you know.

Ignore them, pretend you are an elf.

When they're screaming in your face "Which side are you on?"

And marching with banners saying you must do.

Go down to the stream where the sunlight fairies dream.

Be an elf and do what Elvens do.

All the politicians and the media disgraces

All the gangs of luvvies with their pained and knowing faces

All the virtue signallers signalling for themselves

Bollocks to em, let's be little elves.

Take off your cloak of guilt, put on a magic quilt.

Bollocks to em, let's be little elves.

16.

In Ringling Brothers' Circus there performed an amazing cat.

Assisted by his trainer who wore a ridiculous hat.

A five hundred pound Siberian, one claw could kill a man.

He danced and reversed and curtseyed to the tune of the Big Top band.

The tiger's eyes were orange like his stripes that were not black

For finale he'd prance down the tunnel with his trainer on his back.

One night, in front of two thousand, he bit off the trainer's head.

Then de-limbed three assistants leaving two of them for dead.

The one armed, one legged survivor tried to escape from the cage.

But he opened the gate to the audience and tiger took centre stage.

He killed and maimed a hundred before departing from the tent.

Caught a bus to the town centre with malevolent intent.

For every pub he entered he gobbled down six or seven.

But in larger pubs like Wetherspoons he managed up to eleven.

When the pubs had closed and shut their doors he made for the discotheques

While they were dancing round their handbags he ripped out twenty necks.

"Where can I go at 3 a.m. more humans to devour"

"I know! those all night shopperys like Tesco's 24 hours"

They finally stopped him in Asda, eating the slow Covid queue

Tranquilizer darted him in the neck and took him to Chester Zoo.

The experts there at Chester said "No tiger will be killed!"

But with the use of our "Cricket brainwashing scheme" his brain we can rebuild.

Subject the beast to Cricket for 24 hours a day

Peace, tranquility, leather on willow can be the only way.

Though he has killed six score and seven his murders will all cease

As soon as he sees David Gower standing proudly at the crease.

Every day for five long years it was cricket, cricket, cricket,

Test matches, googlies, off side spins, catches, run outs, wickets.

The day arrived the experts said twas safe to let him go

Cricket had removed his rage and he could rejoin the show.

In the back of the van the tiger thought "Victory!, the experts spout"

"But for me its just the next days play and I'm 127 not out!"

17.

Ghostly Affair. (the things you have to do to exorcise!)

In life I never knew her,

But she was there when I bought the plot.

When the sunlight glints, the wallpaper hints

Of the ever tightening knot.

She lingers for me an invisible,

The corridors hosting her scent.

The smell of damnation, a representation

Of her murderous eternal intent.

Before she became ethereal,

She had lived a long wicked life.

No husband sex drive so she murdered all five,

A truly lascivious wife.

The first she used poison, the second a fire,

The third a long drop down the well.

Methinks four and five would still be alive,

If carbon monoxide had smell.

If I could touch her I would kiss her,

And twirl the dank hair on her head.

Just giving me chance time to kill her,

But too late she is already dead.

All times in the house I am wary,

Of her devious devilish tricks

I don't mind the house being scary,

Just don't want to be number six.

There's a naked phantasm in my bedroom!

Her ghostbusters dangling free.

With black shiny lips and treacherous hips,

Upsurging the ghost lust in me.

And then the impossible happened,

She got what she'd been long waiting for.

When our deep embrace broke she turned into smoke

And shot out through a crack in the door!

18.

From Raffles to a damp couch.

Grey Goose and springwater at Raffles

Courvoisier at the Hyde Park Hotel

Lunch at the Ritz with a bottle of Claret

Remy Martin to finish as well.

Then large Smirnoffs and tonic at the Tory club

And another and another as well

Crown Royals neat at the ladies Retreat

Glenmorangie when the man rings the bell.

Cold quarts of Stella at the Red Lion

Plus a large gin and tonic or two

Carafe of house wine at the Grapes Club

With a nightcap of rare mountain dew.

Some pints of flat bitter before noon time

Washed down with some once salty nuts

Then off to the Legion when pubs shut

Pints of lager and some gin for the guts.

Then a three litre bottle White Lightning

Asda vodka at nine ninety nine

Lie on your back guzzling warm Frosty Jack

And reflect on your social decline.

19.

Woman in a scarf.

Me feyther geet himsel' killed in't Pretoria

And me mother she were nowt but a girl

But she managed to feed us and rear us

Till John Joe took me heart in a whirl.

He worked on't dray waggons deliverin'

Great barrels of ale for the men

To be swallered and gollopped in gallons

In the grandly named dank drinking dens.

I knitted and darn't and I cooked

Wharever worth cookin' we had

Till John Joe went and geet himself killed

In a moment, just gone, like me dad.

Good for me I didn't have no babies

Cos they threw me from lodgin' to't street

And I spent mony a hard freezin nightime

On a   doorstep on owd Brancker street.

Then I geet a job cleanin' and washin'

For a good man, the squire at the hall

Though he never overpaid me a penny

He were straight and ne'er touched me at all.

Me room were a corner in't th'attic

There I served and were called by a bell

I made mi own clothes and I managed

To save a few shilling as well.

Found th'owd squire dead sitting cold in his chair

And I thowt here we go again

Then I found meself, me and mi suitcase

Standin theer in the street in the rain.

Now I live in't last house in a shambles

Rent paid to a man with brown skin

And I don't have a soul I can talk to

'Cept mi cat and she never stays in.

Ahm owd neah and how did that happen?

Locked away down an owd cobbled street

Just me and mi cat and me memories

Ah've been lucky it'll all be awreet.

20.

Original Sin?

If you have done something wrong say your sorry
If you have hurt someone on purpose show regret
You can only be responsible for your own actions
The colour of your skin doesn't make you guilty yet
If you want to live off history research it well
Don't pick the bits that your gang likes to hear
If you've spent your life bullying and hating others
Then its time for you to change and re-appear
As a kinder, gentler person who's learned a lesson
With empathy and take time to understand
But if you've spent your life caring and never hating
Get off your knees and stand up like a man.
If your family made millions out of poverty
If you benefit from crime and evil deeds
Give it back through work in the community
Tend your moral garden, burn the weeds.
Finger pointing, calling names and fixing labels
Only serves to strengthen racist hate
Have a good look at yourself in the mirror
Is what you see a product of your fate.

21.

Opening Time (newish song)

An open door, a rattled glass,

Churchbell rings the welcome chime.

To recreate our youthful past.

We're here at last at Opening Time

No time of day as fine as this.

Whatever that word means it's fine.

I hope and pray that I won't miss,

That first strange kiss of Opening Time.

It's five minutes past eleven.

I've got the first one in my hand.

Number three the feelings plateaued

I forgot what I used to understand.

The same owd lads, the same owd craic,

That jokes still kills me for the seventh time.

What better place on earth to be,

Than on my knees at Opening Time.

22.

Three Stone Witches.

There's three stone witches up on Harrock Hill

Amongst the bluebells and the dancing daffodils

Who knows why the girls were turned to stone.

Maybe there are some things better left alone.

I woke that morning and I saw the light.

Easter morning and the sun was shining bright

The hares were boxing and the time stood still.

So lucky to be living under Harrock Hill.

I needed feeding so I went to town.

Funny when there's not a single soul around.

Nature's blooming and the blackbird sings.

We don't really matter in the scale of things.

Last night pubs and clubs and dancing feet.

Drinking, talking and there's fighting in the street.

Meanwhile Mrs swallow feeds her brood.

Flies the cosmic sunset without platitude.

I needed nothing so I watched the scene.

Funny not a swallow was a drama queen.

Simple majesty exceeding kings.

We don't really matter in the scale of things.

23.

Walking the lonely path without the poison
Today without it is a good day
A day nearer to it is a bad day
Take the prayer to God and mean it
In the morning pray for the right things
Play every minute as they come in and go
You never know
But maybe something good will be in the next one
The silhouetted tree and the spinning sun
The laughing lake with banks of reeds
The simple joys not bought but given
By the higher power not from a mighty tower
Just a flower nodding in the breeze.

24.

He gives down thumbs on YouTube for a laugh
Re-Tweets nonsensical opinions of hate
Fighting fights on Facebook is his craft
3 o clock in the morning isn't late
Hurting people's feelings lights his eyes
Meanwhile his passing life is on the shelf
His keyboard is a weapon to criticise
All the things he could never do himself!

25.

Jinny Green Teeth.

You know I saw her face once but she was low beneath,

The black oily water, old Ginny Green Teeth.

In a cold darkened pond down off Halfpenny lane,

In the depths of the slime the memories remain.

It's her eyes I can never remove from my dreaming,

And the brief glimpse of teeth so sharp, so green gleaming.

Hypnotic the gaze, mesmeric the ways those

Duplicitous tricks to devour young strays.

Not from the village of course but alone,

Young strangers would come and she'd spit out their bones.

So if you wander down late along Halfpenny lane,

When the moon is a madface and there's blood in the rain.

Beware Jack o lanterns floating out round the pond,

When a gentle sound "hello", try not to respond.

When you want to go in and you need to go in,

Please turn little stranger and run like the wind.

26.

The atomic bomb is hiding in the rainbow
And the genocide is hiding in the sea
The fatberg in the sewer
And the monkey on a skewer
The remnants of the human dignity
The murderer is waiting in the daisies
The famine is hiding in the cake
Down the sweetest country lane
All the weeds have gone insane
God seems to have made a slight mistake.

27.

End of the World!
The ancient Mayans were a complex people
Droughted out in 900 AD
Among there amazing achievements
Was their end of the world prophecy
Studying the cosmos and charting the stars
In strange combinations to delve
They worked out the world would come to an end
December 21st, 2012
But our interpretation was wrong it seems
And our modern world of progress and plenty
Will come to an end in just more than a week
21st of June 2020.

I am not joking that's what they said

It's not one of my Saturday rants.

In 9 days the world will come to an end.

Better put on some clean underpants.

28.

You are all Liars.

You make me feel guilty, you make me so torn

For the colour of my skin and the year I was born.

You give me a label, so I stand in line

To hear your false truths as you guzzle fine wine.

You are all Liars

You are all Liars

Why did I believe in you?

I was taught to be humble and listen to everyone.

Manipulators,

You are all traitors

When you make me ashamed

Of being born in this land.

On the pages of papers and the television screen

False news and omissions, salaries obscene.

Political religion, professional con,

The confusion of knowing which side you are on

All the holiest of books have been written by men

To control the masses with a bloody pen

They beat me at school for not following their rules

Then they heard my confession they made me feel like a fool.

I heard all the speeches I read all the books

Looked at different opinions wasted time that it took.

Your words are so sacred, your themes are so grand

With a smile on your face and a fat cheque in your hand.

19.

The Smuggler!!

It was early in the morning, the low boat came to shore.

In a far flung bay in old Galway, it was loaded to the floor.

Rum and strong tobaccy, wine and silk and tea.

The Smugglers Gang as hard as nails

Looked up and espied me.

I was walking to the shoreline, a towel under me arm.

A brand new pair of Speedos on, the ladies for to charm.

Carry on with your smuggling lads, take no heed of me.

For I'm just a budgie smuggler, going for a dip in the sea.

So go and hide your loot me boys and take no heed of me.

For I'm a budgie smuggler going for a dip in the sea!

A pistol shot! A Threatening shout, the Customs men are here.

They arrested all the smugglers and then they came for me.

They looked down at me Speedos said "We'll take a look in there"

"You're free to go" The captain said "As you've nothing to declare"

So they took and hung the smuggler boys and they let me go free.

For I'm just a budgie smuggler going for a dip in the sea.

30.

If I felt like it.

I could plant some trees, I could break your knees,

I could steal your keys, If I felt like it.

I could right some wrongs, I could write some songs,

I could be King Kong's friend, If I felt like it.

I could make bells peal, I could forge pure steel,

I could make you squeal, If I felt like it.

I could tote a hod, I could pray to God,

Buy a foreign sod, If I felt like it.

Hey Mrs what mood are you in tonight?

Shall I wear a ring or a boxing glove?

Why is it we change our minds all the time?

What did your last slave die of was it love?

You could drink my blood, we could fight in mud,

Make me feel so good, if you felt like it.

You could flatter me, you could batter me,

Even make my tea, if you felt like it.

I could buy you a flat, Give you a cat,

Or a baseball bat, If I felt like it.

I could be aloof, I could be shatterproof,

Even sit on the roof, If I felt like it.

(chorus)

Play musical chairs or we could go upstairs,

Or we could act like squares If you feel like it.

You could play hard sell, You could ring my bell,

Or we could fight like hell, if you feel like it.

I could kiss your lips, I could hold your hips,

Have some fish and chips if we feel like it.

We can raise some geese, we could visit Greece

Or we could both have some peace if we feel like it.

31.

She wasn't much of a looker,

But she had a model's physique

He knew he shouldn't visit her,

But his resistance was getting weak.

Because of all the lock down laws

He risked a thousand pound fine.

So he said "Just keep your face mask on,"

"I'll be there at half past nine!"

32.

I spoke so soft to the old Ash tree - I wonder know you me.

And it bent its boughs and shook it's leaves - In a simple honesty.

Then the fragrant air and the giant oak - I wonder have you a soul

Not a soul like your soul but deep within my bole

I have a spark, a spark of something tingling, knowing, sense

I knew the feel of the six inch nails when they used me for a fence

The rusty nails the rotting holes the hurting human dross.

I touched it's bark, still alive, like dead Jesus on the cross.

33.

I didn't know I was working class,

I didn't know I was poor.

Born in a town where the factory smoke,

Drifted out to the bleak dark moor.

I didn't know I was northern,

I didn't know I had a brain.

Just a creature in a cradle gazing through,

The window at the pouring rain.

I didn't know I was English,

I didn't know I was white.

I couldn't understand the dreams that came,

In the darkness of the night.

I didn't know I was a catholic,

I didn't know I had sinned.

I was warm and fed and loved and listened

To the window and the stormy wind.

34.

Men had built a skyscraper out of glass and steel
A nuclear submarine that never slept.
I awed at their magnificence that didn't seem quite real.
Then I looked and saw the uninvolved sunset.
There was a woman with a face fit for a fashion magazine
And a figure that could make you start to sweat
With a Maserati car that could go like a bullet
Then I looked and saw the uninvolved sunset.

35.
I'M NEARLY OLD
I cleaned my teeth with Savlon
Put toothpaste on my sore toe
Poured orange juice on my Shredded Wheat
Where's my glasses no-one knows.
Found my wallet in the freezer
Boots on the washing machine
Getting old isn't getting any easier
I think I'm somewhere in between.
(chorus)
I'm nearly old, I'm nearly there
I can still climb trees and graze my knees
Then I fall asleep in the chair.
I'm nearly old, I'm almost beat
With the spirit of a wild teenager
And slippers on my feet.

I have jeans with real holes in them
Made by wear and not by trend
I still listen to Jimi Hendrix
But I'm in bed for half past ten
My grandkids think I'm ancient
The In-laws think I'm young
I'm in the middle of the generations
All the great songs have been sung.
Just cut down an old oak tree
And tomorrow I'll be flagging a floor
Then I found the note for the vulnerable resident
Sticking out of my front door.
Sixties are the new forties
That is what the trendsetters say
So I'm joining the Hell's Angels
Because I'm younger than yesterday.

36.
Why are killers always beautiful
The tigers and the hawks
Eyes of superior majesty
Where the blood rip psycho walks
Why are the gentle gentle
The victims torn apart
Why are the killers beautiful
And the breakers of your heart.

37.

Don't go out in that wind my love,

Don't go out in the storm.

The children are asleep my love,

And the fire's crackling warm.

The tiles they are a rattling

And the oak trees bending low

There's things out in that storm my love

Things we do not know.

I don't want to go in that wind my love,

I don't want to go in that storm.

It's easy to stay here my love,

When the fire's crackling warm.

But I must go where that wild wind blows,

And I must face that fear.

For if I don't go out in the storm my love,

The storm may come in here.

38.

I walked along Awolowa road,white shirt wet with sweat

To the garage at the crossroads where I bought my cigarettes

An old man lived in a plank hut by the Polo Club gate way.

Where the rich and the important ignored him every day.

I gave him a few of the cigarettes and crisp five Naira note.

I couldn't spend all that I had and he put it under his coat.

There was a body in the river blown up, a grotesque balloon.

The sunlight dyed the water blood.Back to the computer room.

The mighty mainframe rumbled, the window took my eye.

She was naked to the waist, washing from an old stand pipe.

Oblivious in her garden she turned and saw me looking.

Laughed and grabbed her towel and went back to her cooking.

The palm trees swayed to the wind from the Lagos lagoon.

A distant crackling radio played an old Bob Marley tune.

They told me not to wander in that city after dark.

I found a music cafe overflowing in the back car park.

I borrowed an old electric guitar a man with a smile so bright.

And we played and drank and laughed and sang late into the Nigerian night.

39.

They were selling Christ's tears in tiny glass vials.

Thin splinters of wood from the true cross.

Some pilgrims believed what they needed to.

Holy relics, liar makers of dross.

What is love and why do we want it?

Yet giving love is God's golden key,

To happiness in our daily lives.

Instead of loving only me.

40.

Fight in the Chippy (by Lord Byron)

There's a fight in the chippy,

Between a skinhead and a hippy.

Tomato ketchup splattering the walls.

Skinhead grips the hippy's hair,

Hopes to keep him cowering there,

But the hippy just nuts him in the balls.

Why is combat often seen,

In such halls sans haute cuisine?

Does lack of choice inflame the situation?

Do shortcomings of the menu

Instigate the violence venue?

That should have a more alfresco location.

I dragged them both outside.

Sabred their gizzards open wide.

I then rejoined the queue for the food.

If I had wanted fighting chaps,

I'd have ordered chips and scraps,

But since not I found the whole thing rather rude.

41.

Shakespeare owes me a fiver.

Shakespeare owes me a fiver. I lent him one in the pub.

He was down on his luck, had writer's block,

So I helped him out with a sub.

We were drinking our pints in the tap room.

Two wasps were buzzing around.

Shakespeare said "Are those bees or wasps?"

"Can you tell by the buzzing sound?"

"Two bee or not two bee?", I said "That is the question?"

He ran out quick with his pen in his hand.

I think he had indigestion.

42.

Smoked the Painted Sunset.

Smoked the painted sunset through a little cigar

Threw the last remains through the window of my car

Belted down the back road with my heart on fire

Smoke from the exhaust pipe and smoke from every tyre

False cattle stood like puppets in an empty field

Picture after picture of my memories unpeeled

The cloud ships gliding seamlessly across the dying sky

Heart was oscillating off beat for no reason why

Except the bad volcano in the middle of my mind

Shooting stars of magma on the wasted time behind

Skeletons on bicycles haunting every street

Folded sheets of ladies folded lives so neat

Clown fingers scrambling escaping from the grids

Black eyed hard rock dealers selling toffees to the kids

Beard man on a bench with his chips and his hat

Waiting at the bus stop a redundant bureaucrat

Bouncing in the car park an invisible steel band

Moving, driving, dreaming home in lock down land.

43.

Goodnight Little Richard

Crazy fizzbomb of energy

Banging new rhythms on the piano box

Standing and screaming into the microphone

Bad boy with a big head

Wop bop a loo bop a lop bam boom

A genius has left the room.

44.

He took his medals to Cash Converters on the corner,

For 20 quid he sold his pride to buy some wine.

The cardboard doorway is ok when he is drinking.

But the acid cold at night attacks him from behind.

Its a fearful load, its a lightning load,

Keeping straight on the long straight road.

She has her coffee in the same cup every morning.

Looking at the sky she tries to plan her jobs that way.

The nagging pangs that wear away her point of being.

She fights them off and plans a busy day today.

Its a fearful load, its a lightning load

Keeping straight on the long straight road.

The business suit, expensive car and perfect family.

The bloodshot eyes in the rearview mirror on his way.

The pressures building, every deadline getting harder.

Meeting at nine this time he just can't walk away.

Its a fearful load, its a lightning load.

Keeping straight on the long straight road

She's looking fit she's looking good in the long black mirror

Slinky dress and her make up's almost right

Big glass of red she feels a super confidence,

Says, "I won't be the one to make myself a fool tonight"

Its a fearful road, its a lightning load

Keeping straight on the long straight road.

But future has endless horizons and rainbows with pots of gold!

Old Joe has a garden and you want to see his garden!

Now the hidden bottles in his shed are long away.

His life is good, the sun is shining, he is stronger.

Almost a tear in his eye to bless each single day.

Its a beautiful road its a lightning road

Keeping straight on the long straight road.

45.

What's so special about a tie its just a piece of cloth

Spun by a silkworm or eaten by a moth.

If you're wearing one will you never start a fight?

They wouldn't let me into Blightys club last night.

You can't come in here, you're not wearing a tie.

Rules is rules so don't bother asking why.

So I went down an alley took my Y-fronts off.

Wrapped em round my neck, I looked like such a toff.

But the bouncer looked at me like I'd committed a sin.

No chance Beau Brummel you're still not coming in.

If you get imprisoned and your shouting for Huey,

They take your tie off you so you don't commit suey.

But even if your the nicest man on the planet

Without a tie the bouncer's got a face like granite.

Listen pal even when your dead you have to wear a tie

Best bib and tucker in the coffin when you die.

So whether I go to heaven or whether I go to hell

Don't tell me they're checking bloody ties there as well!

46.

BIT LONELY FOR YOU TONIGHT.

I don't miss the M6 roar and I don't miss the train.

I don't miss the slow commute in the early morning rain.

I don't miss the pushing and the shoving

And the success ladder fight.

But I'm a bit lonely for you tonight.

There's a blackbird looking at me

Not a contrail in the sky

A man on a horse said hello to me this morning

Made me happy for a little while

And I don't know why.

The kettle's the same kettle,

The coffee tastes the same,

I thought I heard someone knocking on my door

Just the breeze in the old door frame

Thought you said my name.

47.

This day is the newest day.

The newest day that's ever been.

Not a single human seen

A newer day than this one.

What a privilege, what a chance,

You may partake in this day's dance.

The moon has never been older

The stars have never been colder

Take this day, it's yours for free.

But save a little bit for me.

48.

Pull your weeds, Plant your seeds

While the sun shines let's make hay.

Kiss your plants, drop your pants,

Naked gardening day today.

if you bloomers have gone droopy

And your main stems's looking short

You can be a gardening groupie

Just come out from your carport.

When the Spring comes things get firm

As the juices start to rise

Don't be put off by a little worm

Stand them up with strings and ties

Ditch the Y-fronts burn your bra

Inhibitions you must slay

Passers by will triple if you show your gardener's nipple

Come out it's naked gardening day today!!

49.

"Opera House, Blackpool, Frank Sinatra, Sunday Night"

Summer 1950, Korean war was all the news
Men asleep in deckchairs, cigarettes, a smell of booze.
The trams in all their finery, the piers and tower alight,
Plus "The Opera House, Blackpool, Frank Sinatra, Sunday night."

Baby boom is starting, Rock and Roll begins,
The Golden Mile of decadence, a penny for your sins,
Twirling skirts and trilbys, a knuckleduster fight,
Plus "The Opera House, Blackpool, Frank Sinatra, Sunday Night."

Candy floss stick in the gutter, toffee apples, fish & chips,
Courting couples on the promenade kissing lipstick lips.
Avoid the clunking trams enjoy the Wakes fortnight.
Plus "The Opera House, Blackpool, Frank Sinatra, Sunday Night."

I wish I could have seen it, I wish I had been there,
In the streets to hear him say "Here I could be Mayor!"
The pavements deep with people, the billboards shining bright.
The Opera House, Blackpool,Frank Sinatra, Sunday Night.

50.

Where dat pipe go grandad, grandad why does it rain.

No don't keep sitting down let's run round't field again.

Why's your hair got white bits, why've you got thin lips

Why can I not have chocolate on't same plate as mi chips

No I don't need toilet, I'm a big girl me,

Can I play with your chainsaw, oh I want a wee,

Are you more than a hundred, have you been on a train,

Is bloodyhell a naughty word, can you do that story again,

Grandad can I stand on't roof, do you drink dirty beer,

My dad does, are you asleep, grandad can you hear,

Can we shoot some wabbits, fill me water pistol up,

Can I have a drink please, no that's not my cup,

Grandad can we climb that tree again, I won't tell mi Mum,

When my dad was naughty did you smack his bum,

Grandad can I have some trifle, just a little bit

Can I have a bit more, did you work down pit,

Can I live here grandad, Can we sleep in't trees,

I'm tired grandad, will you take me home now please.

51.

My love left me for an alien

He's taken her to outer space

I sit gazing at the sky at night

While he holds her in a cold embrace.

I never wanted to watch ET

Or Close Encounters of the Third Kind

I was making toast and cocoa

I never knew what was on her mind.

She developed unhealthy interests

In my reflecting telescope

Now I feel like such a dope.

When the knock came to the front door

There was a sound of vibrating craft

I thought its late for a delivery

Now I'm feeling kinda daft

She said go and find a new love get yourself another girl

My new man is out of this world.

I should have realised what was happening

When she wore that silver suit

And a stick mike and an earpiece

I said your looking kinda cute

But my wonder turned to fear and a tear fell from my eye

When she started zooming through the sky.

52.

Back out in the Wind.

We were singing songs we were righting wrongs,

Playing in the clubs and bars.

We were stealing smokes, we were telling jokes,

Strumming on some fancy guitars.

Now its driving me crazy cos I'm being lazy,

Forgive us lord we have sinned.

Put down the remote and pick up your coat,

Its time to get Back out in the Wind.

(chorus) Back out in the Wind, we're back in the wind

Things go wrong when you're in too long

And your brain becomes a bin

And its a little bit great getting home late.

Time to be Back out in the Wind.

Well the years go by some make you cry,

But good times and memories remain.

Just like everyone our good friends have gone,

Nothing can continue the same.

Down the motorway miles with the tears and smiles

To the places where the losers win.

Put on diamond strings and pack a few things

It's good to be Back out in the Wind.

We were playing towns we were slowing down,

And sleeping in the back of the van.

We need a hit and our clothes don't fit

So we tried to make a plan

In the backstreet night under a broken light

In the places where our posters were pinned.

We said we'll start anew under the skies of blue

Time to be Back out in the Wind.

53.

Hard Country Cheese.

I never thought you'd leave me for another

You said you'd been seeing the marriage guidance man

But you'd also been seeing the vicar and the plumber

And that bloke who delivers sausages in his van

You could have told me that I'd become so boring

When you saw me polishing my collection of rare bicycle lamps

You had many other ample opportunities

I only spend weekdays and Sundays mornings admiring my very
rare collection of european stamps

I never thought you'd leave me on a Friday tea time.

We usually have fish and chips and you like mushy peas

I'd warmed the plates up but you didn't come back from the chippy

Now I'm starving and heartbroken and the only thing left in the
fridge is a piece of cheese.

(chorus)

A piece of cheese! Hard Country Cheese

I'm on my knees, with a piece of cheese.

I cut the rind off to reveal the part not covered in green stuff.

Then I grated it with some mustard and a class A drug.

Two bottles of vodka, 14 pints of lager and a small sherry.

I was just starting to forget you when you decided to phone me
from the pub.

"Honey, its me, I just wanted to tell you that I will always love you,

But I've found Johnny and he's got muscles and hair and everything

He's a Supervisor on the dodgems, You wanna see him swinging around on the back of the cars collecting money he's so clever and cute, anyway back to you:

And I'm sorry about the fish and chips but I just wanted to warn you

Don'r eat that cheese in the fridge I injected it with botulism before I left, ciao"

Hard Cheese, hard country cheese,

I'm on my knees hard country cheese.

54.

Watch out for dogs that make no noise when they approach.

Beware gangs of pensioners disembarking from a coach.

Shun the bloke in summer, in the park, in a mac.

Avoid an angry woman with her hair tied back.

Distance yourself from salesmen coming at you with a smile.

If you see a politician wanting votes run a mile.

Ignore headlines on the front page written by a hack.

Avoid an angry woman with her hair tied back.

55.

The earth is such a canvas for our art.

Two separated by a wall of stone.

Impassable, unclimbable, apart.

Forever they were doomed to be alone.

Unhearable, invisible their love.

They found a tiny crack between two rocks.

Enough for stretched out fingers just to touch.

Tingling time stood still in lover's clocks.

The hopeless brief connection of their fingers

Sent shocks of tender feeling to each heart.

That moment's truth in passing time still lingers.

The earth is such a canvas for our art.

Impossible to kiss upon the lips.

Instead they kissed with frozen fingertips.

56.

Spring is in the scent of the breeze

In the hedgerow, in the fields and in the trees

Vivid green shoots in the valleys and the hills

Sun and rain and fragrant daffodils

Father of the cosmos look on us tonight

Father of wrong and father of right

Father of microbes, father of whales

Lord of the unlimited and the fine details

A poison chalice that night you were brewing

Creating us. What were you doing?

Protect the weak and the sick and the frail

The vulnerable ones, don't let them fail

Lord of the germs and lord of the sun

Look after your children when this day is done.

57.

Wash your hands, Clean the table, Clean the windows, if you are able

Wash your hands, Brush the drive, Pinch yourself, You're still alive

Write a poem, write a book, learn a language, learn to cook.

Build a wall, make a bridge, Put clever comments on your fridge

Make some plans then make some more, paint the ceiling, clean the floor

Help someone who is needing help, change a light bulb, put up a shelf

Walk the dog, enchant a frog, carve a goddess from a log

Mow the grass, clear the ditches, introduce yourself to local witches

Plant a tree, plant a bush, eat some food that isn't mush

Go to sleep, love the dawn, select possessions you can pawn

Wash your hands, wash your face, be content with your safe place

Learn to play a magic flute, creep up slowly behind a newt.

58.

The goose, the goose,

The Canada goose. Let loose in virusland.

Enjoying a great freedom he need not understand.

He and his little lady made a nesting on the isle,

Amid the pond, the fronding pond,

They flew four thousand mile.

It only took one heron,

Terror saurus with vultures wings.

To send them hiding in the hedgerow

Poor little, brave little things.

59.

Looked through the window in the frosty morn

There was a goose with steam coming out of its mouth

A waiting of goslings about to be born

All of its brothers had flown down south

But they were returning to see the news

How the roads are empty and the air is clean

No blood in the gutters no empties of booze

Freshness and beauty all there to be seen

The little birds feeding and nesting for young

The blueness of sky no jet contrails hung

The quiet of mercy the creatures at play

Enjoying their moments on this beautiful day.

60.

Why am I not sleeping in real time?

Mind out in the cosmos, a thing.

Dreaming in technicolour.

From a plot by Poe or by King.

Something is rotten in Denmark.

Not a safe place in any direction.

Am I living in some sort of story?

Or working on forms of protection.

Streets are anxiously silent.

Bus stations, train stations the same.

A lit city lit for no reason.

A part in some computer game.

61.

He kissed Medusa on the lips.

One dark and stormy night.

He thought he would have had his chips.

But he kept his eyes shut tight.

You look at her, you turn to stone.

Sorrow is such sweet parting.

He got out of there just in time.

He could feel that it was starting.

62.

Homeless since he left the shelter.

Boozed up in Platt Bridge.

He should have been a belter.

With all his white privilege.

Mum and Dad both alkys.

Nowt but Strongbow in the fridge.

The jammy little bastard.

With his white privilege.

Born skint and died skint.

Did not attend Oxbridge.

Unlike those who make up stupid phrases.

Those who do have privilege.

Keep your sweeping generalisations.

For the sweethearts in your village.

Or take a one day trip to reality.

One day with no privilege.

63.

You know when something you see or hear strikes a bell of memory.

Might just be the sun shining on a white wall

Or a dog barking from a long way away.

A sliver of sweet rain running down your cheek

Or a song that the radio plays at the start of day.

(chorus)

You can't learn it, it was already there.

Electric light down the back streets of your mind.

A lifting of your mood when the wind tracks veer.

Think now you can leave all the bad days behind.

You know if you walk in the early morning,

When your racing brain is still asleep.

And the flowers and tree top leaves send magic direct and deep/

Where you don't need to understand a single thing.

The chimney smokes rises and the old church bells ring.

(chorus)

All my old places have been torn apart.

Still got streets and pubs and life with a broken heart.

But that's just me, new things come to power.

Young people's time, their time for their sacred hour.

I've got memories like stamped and burnished tin.

Or Tony's voice or Larry's mandolin.

64.

Important safety tips: Don't eat bats.

Try not to lick your backside like the cats.

Don't go shopping, things have gone manic.

Avoid the TV news, they love a good panic.

Go for a walk in the spring sunshine

Go home, lock the door, drink some wine.

65.

I don't know a lot but listen for a bit

Not much I love but you are it.

It's fierce out there in this changing world

Some good, some bad with flags unfurled.

Goodness in chains, I'm sure you will free it

The thing is I won't be around to see it

You're pretty as perfection, bright as gold

You're just a little squirt and I am old

Learn from me, I have made mistakes

They start each day when the morning breaks

But I do know a bit about bad and danger

The things to not do, the deceit and the stranger

So listen for a bit while we climb this tree

I'm an old git and you are just three.

66.

The Poison Cup.

Drink and drugs are mini suicides,

They kill the pain of living.

But only for a little while,

Then it comes back unforgiving.

When it's painted in your blood,

And leathered in your hide.

There is no understanding

Of the poison put inside.

But alright is really alright

When you're free and uncontrolled.

Beware that cup, don't pick it up.

Just come in from the cold.

67.

Sugar Stealer

You used to love me like a fool.

Kids were young and still in school.

I feel your memory on the street.

I can only see my walking feet.

(chorus)

Hello time the great healer

Where are you today

My life's a sugar stealer

Blown away.

(chorus)

A vacancy inside my heart

Ever since we've been apart.

Its nice to laugh the pain still stings

Who knows what tomorrow brings.

(chorus)

Most days are normal some are flat.

But every day can't be like that.

The radio plays a favourite song.

Nothing tangible is wrong.

(chorus)

So this is life and life is this.

Haunted by a missing kiss.

At ten o clock the letters came.

Everything remains the same.

68.

Heidi the yodeling slag heap skiier.

She sits on 't slag heap on a Sunday morn

Doesn't matter if its raining, if its cold or warm

When she's siting in the dirt

She wears her knickers round her skirt

Blowing on an Alpine Horn.

Yodel ai ee, Yodel ai, Yodel ai ee, you little nowty bugger.

She likes to nip in't Social for some apres ski

A pint of Irish coffe or a cup of tea

With a bob hat on her head

Rayban shades to knock 'em dead

All the fellers there are on their knees. (yodel)

When its Spring she dances round the town

With flowers in her hair and her face cast down

With a pocket full of frogs

She tap dances in her clogs

And she'll give you a kiss for half a crown. (yodel)

She can ski like buggery down Parbold Hill

When the owd men see her coming it makes them ill

In her tight skiing pants

She puts them in a trance

Then she can moves in easily for the kill. (yodel)

She likes her fondue and her tartiflette

She can eat alpine dainties just like the rest

But when no-one's looking

She'll be in the backroom cooking

Black pudding, egg and bacon on a French baguette. (yodel)

She represented Wigan at the Winter Games

She skated in th'Arena with her hair in flames

With a spangly little belt

And wearing nothing else

They were inundated with insurance claims. (yodel)

So if you're stood on't slag heaps by the setting sun

And if you hear her coming then you better run

As she slaloms left and right

You won't ever win a fight

With a ski stick sticking out your bum. (yodel)

69.

It started when I bit my tongue,
Quite normal to do that.
But then I went and bit my lip,
And commenced to eat my hat.
I had to bite my fingernails,
Then started on my toes.
To spite my face I took a knife,
And then cut off my nose.
I greased my palm and fried it.
Then threw my right hand in.
I can't continue with this diet.
No wonder I am thin.

70.

Most people believe what they want to believe.
Some honest truths make them feel sick.
To sidestep the pain of changing their minds,
It's much better to just cherry pick,
The snippets of news and the papers they read,
To raise credibility's ceiling.
It is always so easy to stick with the gang,
It gives you that warm cosy feeling.

71.

It was still sleeting when the rainbow came.
Unbelievable perfection in it's coloured arc.
It's left base shimmering bright stripe lights.
Illuminating Eccleston rooftops in the gathering dark.

72.

I saw an owd pal the other day
And it seemed like no time at all
Since we were kids running wild
Kicking't casey against the wall.
Ar't awreet? Ahm awreet,
Wharever awreet means.
Me body's in me jumper and mi legs are in mi jeans
Me head's inside me trilby and me feet are in mi shoes.
Ahm awreet and they't awreet and thattle have fert do.
He said he'd been feelin a bit magish,
And they've put him on some pills
But he still gets out there walking
Up and down the lanes and hills.
While we're here and while we're lucky
Not too much stuff to worry about
Got a few aches and wrinkles
But today the sun is out.

74.

Dear Moses part the water for me,

I'm sinking and the sea is getting deeper.

An Old testament hero just like you,

Can help me to avoid the old Grim Reaper.

Moses will you please be my pal.

Only you can telekenesise the sea.

Dear Moses I will believe in you,

If only you would believe in me.

Dear Jesus turn the water into wine,

I'm lonely and I feel like getting drunk.

If we ever share a cell in a prison,

I swear I'd let you have the top bunk.

Dear Jesus please be my pal.

Only you can set my spirit free.

Jesus I will believe in you,

If only you would believe in me.

Dear Satan, what's it feel like being bad?

You're the best or so the scriptures say.

Being who you are it must be hell.

I'll say a litle prayer for you today.

Dear Satan, will you be my pal?

You are one of the few worse than me.

Dear Satan I will believe in you.

If only you would believe in me.

75.

Storm Ciara and Storm Dennis

Its like living in a blender

But to keep with modern times

Next storm should be transgender.

They think up male and female names

Fancy names in all their finery

But to prove our wokeness

Next storm should be non-binary.

A Dallas or a Bobbie a Corey or a Druid

Cool it with the straight names

Our weather is gender fluid.

Let the next storm name itself

For a change, not being funny

With luck it might identify

As April, warm and sunny.

76.

She heard the Oscar winner's lament,

And she knew just what it meant:

Put on your coat, turn off your central heating.

She sat shivering in the dark,

Thinking of his words so stark.

How kind of him to share his time so fleeting.

He walked down off the stage,

He was really all the rage,

Back slaps and champagne flutes, a crazy scene.

In his two thousand dollar suit,

He threw his Oscar in the boot,

Then rode home in his five litre limousine.

77.

Views from the loo. (a fragment)

My friend can see Ingleborough whilst having a shower.

But only in winter when the trees aren't in flower.

From my toilet seat standing, reaching up for a spell.

If visibility is gracious I can just see Scafell.

There's a fellow in Nepal tries his level best,

But from no bathroom appliance can he see Everest.

But a strange Indian lady as she sits on her loo

With luck and two mirrors she can make out K2.

Maybe citizens of Pompeii, had they been more curious,

Got bath advance warnings from the smoking Vesuvius.

So when designing a bathroom forget about leaks.

Just ensure you can savour any prominent peaks.

78.

Mistakes and regrets, things that can't be undone.

Ashes and cinders from a love that was burning.

Down the old lanes and the days of the sun.

To the fork in the road where you took the wrong turning.

Decisions of life, some are easy some hard.

Some that may leave you with a forever yearning.

For what could have been and what should have been,

At the fork in the road where you took the wrong turning.

So here we are now and a new day unfolds,

On a unique life full of mystery and learning.

Enjoy every moment, so precious, forget,

The fork in the road where you took the wrong turning.

79.

Pint of black mild on a cast iron legged table.

Half a Park Drive balanced in the ash tray.

Arthritic fingers still wrapped up with hard skin.

He could pick up that table with his teeth in his heyday.

Broken fists covered with curves of scar tissue.

A few round his eyes and a list to his nose.

Invisible view through the wall in the distance.

Boots polished black and a crumpling of clothes.

Nowt left of the old pals, the grafters the jokers.

Nowt left of the raging and the bully boys slain.

He's back on the wet street, surrounded by nonsense.

A hard man of old walking home in the rain.

80.

There's a new shop opened down our way, I think its called Subway.

I'm not on a diet so I though I would try it

Chicken roll and coffee and watch the world go round.

What could possibly go wrong?

She said what sort of chicken, I said that bird that clucks around pickin'

Little bits of corn from off the floor

She said Mister in this venue we've got a very extensive menu

Then she looked at me and she looked towards the door.

So I sat down at a table I said can you tell me what's available

She sighed and then she looked right in my eyes:

We got chicken wings and chicken breast, chicken legs if you like them best

Pizzacola chicken and then there's chicken Tikka

Rotisserie and chicken bacon melt, Some so hot you'll need to wear a seat belt,

Sliced or shredded, cold or hot, Eureka!

Then do you want a roll or a bun or a slice?

9 grain multi seed is rather nice

Hearty italiano or gluten-free she boasted

9 grain wheat or chilli paprika, some strange stuff from Cost rica

And do you want it toasted or untoasted?

Next comes the salad we got Jalapeno

Caesar salad or salad Philipino

Tomatoes, red onions,black olives and pickle with glaze.

We got crispy onion and diced beetroot

Mixed peppercorns and fresh bean shoots

But they are only available Fridays and Saturdays.

Then of course the toppings Garlic Avioli, Hickory smoked BBQ and Mexican chilli,

Tomato ketchup, HP sauce and vinaigerette.

Chipotle southwest and Piccalilli, Vegan light Mayo and sticky sweet chilli

And of course sea salt and pepper, don't forget.

Now you mention coffee, it's not that simple,

She screwed up her eyes and her forehead wrinkled,

Listen closely buddy these are what we've got.

We got Piccallolo Latte and Latte Machatto

Long white, short black, white Americano

Espresso, flat white, Cappucino, cold or hot.

She drummed her nails on the counter and looked at me

There was queue behind me it was quarter to three

I think she was mad and she was ready to get lippy.

I put on my hat and I put on my coat looked her in the eyes and cleared my thoat.

I said thanks very much but I think they've just opened the chippy...

81.

New Love Song.

You are a stunning beauty , there's no doubt.

You have style, you have charisma, you have clout.

Your face has been seen on every fashion magazine.

From New York to Paris and every city in between.

Your work on world good causes is renowned.

At the noblest charity dinners you'll be found.

In your bin discarded scripts for the top A film parts.

At your feet the fading memories of a thousand broken hearts.

You're world renowned and loved for all to see.

But here's a heartfelt message from me:-

You little shit, you little shit.

Everything obnoxious you are it.

First time I've met a creature with not one redeeming feature

Your entrails should be boiled in a pit.

You little shit, you little shit.

I hope the vultures eat you bit by bit.

From the day your Mum gave birth you have tainted Mother earth.

You little shit, you little shit, you little shit.

82.

I see things

Some things I shouldn't see

Then some things

Ignite the fire of creativity

I must be soft

To survive and guard

Stop seeing things

And make me hard

But if I stop

And just pretend

The things I see

Will never end

83.

Zip it Shakespeare! You have nothing to say.

You're a privileged white man at the end of the day.

Same goes for Milton, Dryden and Wordsworth,

I'd sing out your praises but it's more than my jobs worth.

Shut up Bob Dylan and you Leonard Cohen,

Paul Simon, white jews? There is no way of knowin.

Pack it in Marlowe and Shelley and Blake,

Chaucer and Hardy you made a mistake.

Frank Whittle, Faraday and A G Bell,

Stephenson and Baird and Darwin as well

In this new kind of racism where talent is thin

You are still being judged by the colour of your skin.

(Forgot Newton sorry)

84.

Does Gnasher know he's a dog?
Does Genoa know she's a cat?
Why do you think you're a human?
Did somebody tell you that?
Your ego, your body, your thinking,
Your creations, your love and your face?
You're just a tight cluster of atoms,
Colliding with others in space.

85

Me mother give me a spit wash
And ran her hand through me hair
Told me to pull me socks up
Then realised the odd pair.
Wiped me nose with her hankie
Told me to zip up me flies
Tutted at me braces and short pants
Both of them the wrong size.
Looked at the scrapes on me best shoes
And did up the knot in me tie
Have a good first day at Cambridge
She said with a tear in her eye!

86.

Top o' Church street rainy bus stop, waiting for the 313.

But the 16 came and I got on that, it was all the same to me.

Going south to't youth club, group on on a Wednesday night.

Drink some pop and have some chats, watch Daffy have a fight.

Kissed a girl under strobing lights, her breath it smelt of cider.

Who knows when you are 16, what's going on inside her.

87.

The days of old.

There used to kings and princes right

In the days of old in the days of gold.

At the head of their armies they used to fight.

In the wonderful days of old.

There used to be dragonflies three foot wide.

When they beat their wings they could turn the tide.

There used to be maidens pure and fair,

With yellow teeth and filthy hair.

In the days of old in the days of old

You were scared of god and you didn't spare the rod.

And if you lived down by the sea you could eat fresh monsters for your tea.

Your clothes were rank and your armpits stank,

In the wonderful days of old.

Young men volunteered to fight.

They knew they'd win cos they were right.

There were Douglas fir trees 500 foot.

There were just too big they had to be cut.

There used to be handsome men back then.

They stunk worse than a wild boars den.

In the days of old in the days in the days of old.

You were already old when you were 10 years old.

And if you lived up in a tree you could eat wild owls for your tea.

Times were nice and you were covered in lice.

In the wonderful days of old.

88.

She has a spider in each armpit
And a scorpion up her nose.
She has "death" and a pretentious latin word,
Tattooed on her toes.
She has a suicidal budgie,
And a terrapin called Frank.
She has fourteen pounds and fourpence
In savings in the bank.
She lives inside a narrow house.
Not much wider than the stairs.
She's an interesting lady.
But no-one really cares.

89.

I awoke there with the sun, black crows were squawking.
What better time to spend than go dog walking.
My little dog is fair, she loves me cos I'm there.
How lucky on this day to be a human.
Rabbits scuttering from our path, the streams were twinkling.
Through the wet grass of the fields the fox was slinking.
My dog in beast disguise looks sweetly in my eyes
How lucky on this day to be a human
Magic moment spied a hare! its ears were twitching
Nature's green in glorious view the woods were witching
My dog she licks my face she loves me for her life.

How lucky on this day to be a human.
Far beneath fine Harrock Hill, the views were dancing.
There the sheep and little lambs in joy were prancing.
My dog she keeps me safe from all the worlds disgrace
How lucky on this day to be a human.

90.

Time drips from the clocks
Slides down the gutters
Into the river and sails away
How do I know?
Nobody saw it go.
Another day.

91.

Hot as a river of blood here
Nice to coldly disappear
Under the castle walls of stone
Sitting for some moments all alone
Looks like the grids have never seen rain
Temporary image - rains come again
Just now the road is lined with dust
I must contain myself, I must
Unartable sunset, outside the range
Of a painters brush or a mind deranged.
We are the ones with brains like freaks.
It'll be different in a couple of weeks.

92.

Wish I could wander down the old streets
In the old towns in the old days.
Before my time came there was a world before
That is not the same.
To see the stone streets and the grand pubs
And the cheap signs.
Wish I was able in that dreamworld
To solve a little mystery in my old brain.

93.

He loved it, that Martin guitar,
He went to London to buy it.
He could play like a whizz anyway,
But they let him sit and try it.
He brought it home on the train,
To play for his beloved to hear.
But she didn't care, she was having an affair,
And a move up in career.
When he found out he picked her up
By the neck and smashed out her life.
Splinters and strings and unplayed things,
The guitar, not his wife.

94.

"15 quid for the cello!" said the mildly amenable fellow.

"20 quid for the drum", said the bloke with the wobbling bum.

"2000 for the Persian rug" said the seller with eyes like a bug.

"50 million for this painting!" said another without fainting.

"How much for the girl?", said he with the moustache twirl.

"She's 15 and she's thin, so I'll throw her brother in"

"I can only offer 20 but I'll stretch to 25"

"I'll be back on Sunday if you can keep them both alive"

How much in the desert will you pay for a block of ice.

Everything has a value and everything has a price.

95.

I bought Sequoia saplings from the web.

Three delivered sticks near to dying.

Dried out in the paper envelope.

Plucked out quick just cos I was buying.

I see the blizzard trees the ones who have

Withstood persistent fierce wind for ages

Mighty oaks and beeches and the firs.

Old age and beauty while the nature rages

Those little things I bought, the little twig,

When I am old and gone they will be beautiful and BIG. X

96.

I used to love your atoms.

I met you on that fateful night

Our love was at the speed of light

Opposites attract - love at first sight

But in physics all things must pass

You told me that you really cared

That E equals M C squared

Our atoms were uniquely paired

But ergo - our love has no mass

Emotionally we romance and revel

But broken down to sub atomic level

You were just a lying little devil

No energy - our love has no mass.

97.

There's a hint of winter in the air.

Little birds are feeding everywhere.

There's a mist that hangs around the streetlights

Last rose has given up her fight.

There's a tang of ocean on the breeze.

Little whirlwind spins the falling leaves.

There's a fire crackling in the hearth tonight.

Makes me feel that everything's alright.

(chorus)

You come and go, You come and go,

From the dusty, sunny days to the icicles and snow.

We live your hands, You live in our hands.

There's a hare staring into nowt.

His savage brain can work the seasons out.

There's a robin, braver than a knight.

Patrolling th'hedgerow before the fading light.

There's a hawk on't barbwire with his rags.

Little fieldmouse dead upon the flags

In't soil a cheeky new young daffodil

While December is raging in the hills.

(chorus)

There's a black bud pointing to the sky

Little water in the corner of my eye

Empty can of Stella thrown into the ditch

Invalidates the spell of nature's witch.
There's an oak tree dying limb by limb,
A million insects living off his skin.
Mother Nature keeps me as her pet.
Walking home forever in her debt.

98.
Its so easy to fall in hate
Especially when you don't feel too great
When your self love is in danger
Always better to blame a stranger
Its so easy/my loss your albatross
It's so easy to be a lazy thinker
Especially when the question is a stinker
When your life's left on the shelf
Take it out on someone else
Its so easy/my inability your liability
When your heart has felt a pang
Go and join a hateful gang
Your life is stretched by ropes and pulleys
Don't deal with it just join the bullies.
Its so easy/my silence their violence.

99.

That pound that you gave to the beggar today

Was used before you in a paedophile's pay

To lure a young teenager with a bottle of cider

Your good pound was used to put bad things inside her

The week before that the same pound played a part

In giving a sick person a new working heart

Then it was used in a hot headed flutter

On an 10/1 runner by a gambling nutter

Last year as it found itself in a bank

It was part of a huge sum to build a war tank

Then, wonder of wonders, it wound up in church

Thrown in the collection from a deep pocket search

Before that, along with a pile of it's mates

It paid to put food on some poor people's plates

Then it was part of a payment to buy

Some bags of white powder from a dubious guy

But this idea from Werner may seem different and strange

He said there's no memory or conscience within your loose change!

100.

I loved you the first time you hit me

I saw that calm look on your face.

Your eyes that signified nothing

I knew I'd found my deserved place.

Being smacked around just for no reason

It helps me get used to my fear.

Especially at this festive season

When you've had a few rums with your beer.

Thank you for making things special.

I'll scrape your dinner off the wall.

I'll clean it up better I promise

As I hear the door slam down the hall.

101.

Lower Broughton wants me Lord I can't go back there (repeat)

I'm banned from all the pubs in Salford.

If a man ever needed chinning he did.

No-one has the right to say what he said in that pub.

He said that Bolton Wanderers are a crap club.

Then he started turning nasty, I hit him in the face with a red hot pasty.

Then I jumped into a taxi

In it was a woman who said her name was Maxi

She was drinking special brew all on her jacksy

Can you tell me where there's some cheap digs.

She said "Here you bas****" and she punched me in the ribs.

I panicked when I heard machine guns gunning

I jumped out and hit Langworthy road running

I thought I'd need to use a bit of cunning

We'll move to the EU live in Brussels

Me and you and our Jack Russells.

102.

So you fell off your horse and it hurt.

Do you remount or just give up riding.

The old days are gone and the new ones are here.

Your steam train is stuck in the siding.

Nobody cares what you think anyway.

Not really, that have their own reason.

Just walk in the rain and face out the storm.

Kick start your brain, a new season.

103.

Dear Witch

Forgive my intrusion but can you fix me an infusion

That will part the curtains of my dreams?

Something black and bubbly

If not too intensely troubly

For you to find one in your book of schemes.

One long black fingernail can turn the pages

While the fever in my heart's dark rages

The beauty of your ugliness engages

With dusky desires of my wicken soul.

Make it calm my boiling blood

Grind it from the blackest bud

And put it in an unblessed bowl.

104.

My pals are trees and dogs

Pussy cats and frogs

The Moon and shooting stars

Pheasants dodging cars

Squirrels, rabbits and bats

Not too keen on rats

Hope they don't bear grudges

Don't appreciate budgies

Being locked in cages

Pay the budgies wages!

Let the budgies free!

Put them on a three

Day week. They have suffered enough

The little blue balls of fluff

Budgies playing a waiting game
Have you no shame
Put down that banjo
And let the budgies go!!
In an ongoing freedom debate situation
At least give them a brief vacation
Don't be so bloody rotten
let them fly round the room on a piece of cotton ...Noooo!

105.

I saw the abandoned man
Dirty blanket and an empty can
In the alley where the cold rain ran
I kept on walking.
I saw the splitting shoes
Ragged coat, stale smell of booze
Eiderdown of daily news
I kept on walking.
I saw the hopeless look
My cheap change that he took
In his pocket a worn out book
I kept on walking.
I was stamped with guilty on my head
Better living there better dead
I could have offered him a bed
I kept on walking.

106.

Trying to help in the Asda?

As she bent over the frozen food section,

The sight of her caused an awkward inflection,

In my voice. She was choosing her favourite tipples.

Standing proud in the coldness her raspberry ripples.

Three packets of gum,

A bottle or rum,

I tried to help, grabbed her two tins of Chum.

I was out of my wits,

As she near did the splits,

I tried to assist taking hold of her bits

That fell onto the shiny white floor

Before being escorted out of the door?

Why?

107.

If I smoked I'd smoke one now.

Light it, hold it in my fingers.

Watch the blue smoke drift away,

While the last light lingers.

If I drank I'd drink one now.

Passing poison through my blood.

Then another just in case,

Somebody finds something good.

If I cared I would care now,

While heart and brain are still engaging.

Mediocrity haunts the walls,

Yellow moon in silent raging.

108.

The irrelevant elephant lived for tricks.
Despite his master's nasty kicks,
The whips, the anger, the sticks.
His voluminous body had no point,
His giant form only to perform,
The tricks that made the people laugh.
His smiling master the psychopath.
Then when the audience paid and left,
The irrelevant elephant chained and caged,
His slow big brain became enraged.
His strength to rip the rings of steel.
Snap the unbreakable bars of steel.
The caravan swayed the giant beast pushed,
The caravan over and over crushed,
Turned the trainer into bloody mush.
Then standing there in a gentle trance,
He regarded his irrelevance.

109.

I walk the cliff path.
Precarious, steady steps.
Not too fast.
Don't look down, or up too much.
Mindful of each step.
And the steepness of the fall.
The whizzdom of the world passes me by.
There are little flowers here.

110.

Hello today you are the furthest point ever in the future.
Every other day is past and unchangeable.
As Shakespeare said:
"What's done is done".
But today is strangeable.
Riding the future wave by the second.
Let me help it to be different.

111.

There's a lost dog in the wind and no-one really cares
While she walks along the road in the cold black night
The cars go whizzing past and she sniffs the alien air
Trying to find that place where everything's alright
Poor lost dog in the wind just tipped out of a car
Confused, she runs, all that she can do
Trying to find a something that she cannot understand
Come here little thing just me and you.

112.

When time was, I was clean
As clean as a clean machine.
When time was, I thought I knew,
Things about me and you.
When time was I was almost innocent,

Not realising my selfish intent,
Thinking love for your fellow man,
Was enough to carry me through,
To the perfect days of me and..... me.
Now I see screaming faces in upside down plug sockets
My ideas in other people's pockets.
When time was.

113.

I can't change
I tried but I can't change prophetic
The unique stamp
The blood brain of genetic
To change a little bit though
Skilled screws to put the ball on pace
On a trajectory to a better place
It was done before I came
Opportunity to shed the blame
I am part of that but now a clown
A horrid face
The black ball going down.

114.

Sky was green and yellow,
Tree silhouettes dry black.
Rare good times were flying west,
They were never coming back.
Fields were flat and frozen,

My thoughts were icebox blue.
Final days were chosen,
For the end of me and you.
Orange lights were twinkling,
Along the old By-Pass.
Emptiness was empty,
As empty as this glass.

115.

On planet Zog
There is a bog
Bigger than Indo-China.
In terms of mud
There is m'lud
Nowhere that is finer.
On planet earth
There is a dearth
Of places quite so sticky.
Unless you count
The large amount
Of filthy Politicky.

116.

Question everything you are confronted by lies,
Look after your children, never fear.
The ordinary man in the street will never die,
Don't wait for the future it is here.
They're fighting in the streets fang and tooth
Hitting baseball bats like Babe Ruth
We would just like to be told the true truth
Why am I yelling? - what are you selling?
Question everything, burn all newspapers now,
Throw a big brick through your new TV.
Yellow vest are visible, the bankers are invisible,
The rulers never want you to be free.
Question everything, but don't fall in hate,
Love your fellow man from all the earth.
Why is all the money in the hands of the few,
Its getting worse, its getting worse, its getting worse.

117.

In love with a rare butterfly.
On my wall you exquisite little thing.
Will you accept from me this diamond ring.
Sunlight passing through your delicate artful wings.
But if you loved me too there would be things
That would make it hard for us to be a pair.
Parts of our lives so difficult to share.
For all relationships have troughs and peaks.
But I think you only live about two weeks.
Show you to my mates, they drink the dregs,
They'd make jokes about you having those six legs.
We'd have to make the most of precious time.
To love each other while we're in our prime.
So you sit there, stop flitting around.
And I'll just look and try to be profound.

118.

Ordinary murder.
He wanted back the twenty quid he'd lent her.
If she didn't give he said he'd cut her.
They were arguing outside the closed Jobcentre.
A piece of paper floated down the gutter.
The point of the afternoon was missing.
A bloke was leaning on a red car bonnet.
She crumpled like a puppet, rain was hissing.
Double decker bus went past, three people on it.

119.

Had to let the chauffeur go, bloody pranged the Rolls again.
And Fritz, my German butler, is driving me insane.
He's forgotten his main duty is managing Chez Berry.
Instead he thinks that I don't know he's stealing my best sherry.
Cook is ruddy hopeless, the caviar's all runny.
But if I point this out to her she thinks I'm being funny.
The gardeners, oh the gardeners, please don't get me going.
Too old and slow and don't you know there's a weed in the lawn
and its growing!
I've had enough of staff today, I'll give them all the sack.
Get on the bloody phone and get that Melanie woman back.

120.

Ghost pubs of the A6
Dead under orange street lights
Empty car parks, boarded doors.
I'm missing you tonight.
Daft to think it matters,
It probably never did.
They were a place when stuff gets hard I hid.
Ghost pubs of the A6
big nights piano banging
Weeds in the gutters
Signpost hanging.

121.

Look at the state of her
Legs up to her arse
Tattoos emerging from her knickers
What a bloody farce!
Look at the state of him
With his sandals and his beard
Thinks he's a bloody professor
He just looks weird
Look at that daft bugger
With his handbag and his eye gloss
Prancing around enjoying himself
Like he couldn't give a toss.
Why's she trying that on for?
No chance it will fit.
Look at me. Oh shit.

122.

I don't feel like leaving.

I don't feel like grieving, I don't feel like leaving,
While the wind is warm and dry and the view still loves my eyes.
I don't feel like weeping, I don't feel like sleeping.
Not sure what I'm supposed to do. Just now I don't want to be like
you.

Bobo bought me a whisky and I threw it in his face
He said You should be ashamed of yourself
You're a disgrace man, a disgrace.

(chorus)

Old men behaving badly, you should be acting your age.
Go and penance sadly, Go and get back in your cage.

(chorus)

The Imam told me life is not for fun. The priest he said the same.
I just looked up at the sun, We're still in the glory days.

(chorus)

123.

The amazing handbag of mystery.
Mary Poppins had a handbag that could hold a standard lamp.
It's capaciousness has gone down in history,
But even Poppin's bag has to take a second place
Behind my wife's amazing handbag of mystery.
Her handbag of mystery contains her purse and keys,
E-cig, pens and pencils and her glasses.
Papers and receipts, screwdrivers and files,
Tickets, cards, stamps, more keys and passes.
I-pad, Kobo, I-phone a pack of chewing gum
Cheque book and letters from the bank.
A little funny piece of iron, some dog treats and a brush,
Instructions how to start a Sherman tank.
Address books and a novel, a little set of spanners,
Maps, a tyre inflator and nail clippers,
Some loose change and a flick knife
A pacamac, a hand grenade and some slippers.
The further in you go the larger it becomes.
Eventually finding everything ever lost.
Secret compartments that link with outer space.
But enter at your peril and your cost.
If I ever have the cheek to look into that bag
Its like breaking into Fort Knox gold bank vault.
And if there is one tiny thing a millimetre moved
It will always, always, always be my fault!

124.

Beethoven was never deaf.
He was getting tired of what he wrote.
So he pretended to be deaf.
Just to get the symphony vote.

125.

Einstein stole my slide rule.
He thought he was ever so smart.
Then he made up Relativity.
The grey haired Austrian tart!

126.

Under the Testicle tree.

Well I ain't much of a scientist but I know where babies come from.
Me and Candice-Marie were walking home from a night at the
senior prom.
Now Candice-Marie is a good church girl and with her its no ifs and
no buts.
But when she looked at that tree then she looked at me
And said "Look at the size of them nuts!"
I want to be under the testicle tree, just you and me under the
testicle tree.
When the moon and starlight falls we'll be sitting there under green
dangling balls
I want to be under the testicle tree.
Me and Candice-Marie got married, we got 14 kids of our own.
But when they make a racket we put on a jacket and go for a stroll
all alone.
With the birds and bees and the walnut trees where the beautiful
butterfly flits.
Our favourite place so we find a space Surrounded by the dangly
bits.
I'd like to be etc.

127.

The iron bridge is rusting in the drizzly wind.
Victorian cast iron riveted junctions.
Straight and true with bits falling off for a long time.
Sleeper planks rotting and crumbling into Middlebrook.
Floating bit by bit to oblivion towards Bolton.
Courting couples and picnic families.
The old bridge carries the souls of memories.
Working men spitting in the breeze on the trains below.
A sugar stealer passing through a place where once stood strength.

128.

Would You Save My Soul.

If I sold my house, if I sold my land,
If I gave everything away except the clothes I stand in.
If I tried so hard to understand,
No selfish pride, no earthly goals,
Would you save my soul.

(chorus)

Would you save my soul Lord, would you save my soul.
It's a heavy load, it's a lonesome road and I'm feeling old.
In the dark sad night still the stars shine bright
Through my weary eyes and my begging bowl
Would you save my soul.

(chorus)

If I change my ways and I make a stand.
Spend a little time just helping out my fellow man.
If i try so hard to understand.
With a piece of love like a burning coal.
Would you save my soul.

(chorus)

When the wind is cold and the road is rough
I look up into the sky but it's not enough
So I try so hard to understand
Instead of spinning down into a dark black hole
Would you save my soul.

(chorus)

129.

Saints and Super Freaks..

One night in the garden of Eden, Adam and Eve started breedin'
An innocent pursuit potentially, but their offspring grew
exponentially.
If we were all invented by god, he must have been asleep on the
job.
But if we are descended from the monkeys, that explains political
power junkies.
Don't believe what they say on the news.
Don't make sense its probably not true.
When they point to the books on their shelf.
Just always be true to yourself.
Unable to contain our intelligence, we resorted to art and
belligerence.
Built pyramids that outgrew the sky, while around us the poor
creatures die.
We can hardly get through a night, without hating or creating a
fight.
Like a hen house with a billion pullets procreating like machine gun
bullets.
Beware of the city elite, they will steal ground from under your feet.
Explain that its your turn to pay, While they keep theirs and give
yours away.
We are saints and killers and crooks, readers and the writers of
books.
While the rivers are full of blood and fat, How did we get to that?
We are scientists, lawyers and geeks, we are born to be the super
freaks
Drinking poison from a rusty can give your last penny to a starving
man.
(Don't believe what they say etc.........)
I used to be a two gallon gulper, Mea culpa, mea maxima culpa.
But now when the sweet day is done, I like to set like the setting
sun.

130.

Some dogs, cats and people are scared of the storm,
When loud claps of thunder fear fills you.
There is nothing to worry about thunder my friend,
It is always the lightning that kills you.

131.

I've shelved my plans for invading North Korea,
Even though their chance of beating me is zero.
Sometimes you've got to let the others have a go,
And I'm getting tired of always being a hero.
I've returned my Nobel Peace prize for literature
At the risk of being seen some a sort of villain.
But prizes and certificates and awards and such,
Are for lesser men like Mandela and Bob Dylan.

(chorus)
Its nice to be nice , its OK to be OK.
You don't have to be a winner to enjoy each lucky day.
We have inescapable lows, or seek artificial highs,
Sometimes its just alright to be alright.

I've decided not to enter Mister Universe,
Even though this year I have a real chance.
Cos the winner always seems to come from planet earth,
And you want to see my dead tight training pants.
I've declined an invitation from The Voice UK.
Though its obvious my victory was nigh.
Cos when my wife can hear me singing in the bathroom
She always looks like she is going to cry.

(chorus)

When will that Kate Winslet leave me alone?
Her and Angelina Jolie, bloody hell!

Either waiting for me outside Yates's Wine Lodge.
Or banging on my door and ringing't bell.
No! Eric Clapton, I can't give you a lesson,
You'll have to learn C minor on your own
Anyway you can't be good at everything
And I think I've got a headache coming on.

132.

Like a Lancashire missionary
Taking niceness and black puddings to the south
Flat vowels, uneven teeth in his mouth
Poverty stricken, skinny little boy
Grown on chips and simple joy
From a dirty cup
But reaching Euston looking up
His new job made him start to think
Even the words Wednesday and Thursday
Created reasons in his mind to have a drink.

133.

-459.67 Fahrenheit is absolute zero
You can't get colder than that
When atoms stop moving
And life stops improving
Don't take off your hat.

134.

Its nice to be nice,
Its ok to be ok.
You don't have to be fantastic
To enjoy each lucky day.
The inescapable lows,
The artificial highs,
Sometimes you just know,
When everything's alright.

135.

Hot as a river of blood here
Nice to coldly disappear
Under the castle walls of stone

Sitting for some moments all alone
Looks like the grids have never seen rain
Temporary image - rains come again
Just now the road is lined with dust
I must contain myself, I must
Unartable sunset, outside the range
Of a painters brush or a mind deranged.
We are the ones with brains like freaks.
It'll be different in a couple of weeks.

136.

Sunset Sonnet

A vacuum of stillness hosts the silence.
A rotting branch fallen upon the grass.
The house is looking tired the slates are split.
All pieces of our lives will surely pass.
There is no such thing as perfect loving,
As tides recede by moonlight so we part.
The love that people lie about in bed,
Or bars with poison pumping round the heart.
Lend me a fiver now, I need a drink.
A bench, a bag, a bottle and some time.
Don't really care just now what people think.
I want to be with losers in their prime.
The winning and the losing, keeping score.
Is nothing, really nothing any more.

137.

White Crow.
I saw the white crow in the vivid morning,
Wearing a blazing suit shimmering in the sun.
The other crows seemed not to notice him,
Strutting and prancing all as one.
His white was whiter than white.
Their black a mysterious irradiance.
They played and fought together in their crow world.
I could hardly tell their conspicuous difference.

138.

Everybody walks different.
Everybody talks different.
They all have different thoughts from you and me.
Everybody feels different.
Everybody looks different.
I can't understand a single one you see.
We can read the same words.
We can see the same things.
Unravel all in pieces in our brain.
But my eyes filter
And my brain filters
And what's left is mine and yours is not the same.

139.

Ode to a shit day.
Give thanks above for this diurnal farce,
This day's as pretty as an earwig's arse.
Mother nature's going to get a slap,
For covering up the sky with this grey crap.
Bollocks to the sun, the two faced git,
Not even one face shown, this days so shit.
The nicest thing this bloody day revealed?
A flock of shitehawks landing in the field.

140.

Most people are normal and nice
And don't act like hyperactive vultures.
But nasty people do bad things.
Depending on their cultures.
Badness has its stereotypes.
Local ways to make disgrace.
For example an English football hooligan.
Will headbutt you in the face.
I try not to do that too much now.
I just create my own mystique.
Useful if you can't stand violence.
And have a poet's physique.

141.

You know that bloke, that hero bloke,
Rescued you in a dinghy.
Everybody knows him, what's he called?
Err Thingy.
Who's that chef, that master chef,
Makes that cheese stuff very stringy.
He's been on telly loads of times.
You know him, Thingy.
That glamour model, I can see her face,
Her bits have gone all swingy,
She got married to that famous actor,
Bloody hell, Thingy!
My memory may have left me,
But my beloved is quite clingy.
We love each other very much.
Don't we, err, Thingy?

142.

Its dark over the deep.
Bright in tinsel town tonight.
The beating city diesel fumes and stray scent of a burnt onion
hotdog.
Sirens, engines, alarms, shouting, anger at the taxi queue.
Stink of stale beer and vomit.
Then
Here in the forest to sleep with the trees.
With nature's creatures.
Not in the palaces of men.
No need to sleep with one eye open then.
Not your ideologies, nor your political wings.
Not your factions, groups and belongings.
Not your anger, pride all counterfeit.
I don't want any part of it.
The silence of sleep.
Its dark over the deep.

143.

(Draft of a comedy song about Brexit)

When the planes stop flying from London to Rome
And they brick up the tunnel to France.
When the ports are blockaded and the doors are all locked
Our neighbours won't give us a chance.
No wine on the shelves, we must make it ourselves.
No big German cars in the queues
How will we survive the rest of our lives
Outside of the great EU.

No more skiing weekends in Val D'Isere.
Its the Pennines for you now my dear.
A few games of whist when you are off piste,
And a pie and some crisps with your beer.
We used to like visiting Paris.
Walk the Champs Elyses in a shower.
Now forget the Eiffel, sit down to some trifle,
Underneath Blackpool tower.

(chorus)
So we're all preparing for Brexit
My wife has been stockpiling wine
The couple next door made a hole in the floor
Installing their own plonk pipeline.
There'll be no more orders from Brussels
No more rules from the EU elite.
But the first thing is clear when the smoke disappears
Kick Teresa right out on the street.

Well we managed before and we'll manage again
You don't have to go down on your knees.
There's a bloke round the corner who makes his own booze.
And his wife makes a nice bit of cheese.
And you don't have to go to places remote
To enjoy the sunshine and sand.

Get off at the station use imagination
Fleetwood can be rather grand.

I've bought a brand new Nissan Micra
Got ride of the Mercedes Benz
Its not quite as quick but I've learned a new trick,
Its too small to pick up your friends.
You can get a nice croissant in Tesco's
Or a Taramasalata flavoured Whippy
And exotic choices in the ordering voices
Are heard at our own local chippy.
So don't get too worried about leaving.
You don't have to live in a bunker.
From Blackpool to Leeds it'll fulfil your needs
And you won't have to ask that bloke Junker.
We'll still have in Continent neighbours
So lets just all give it a chance.
Just work harder together and face the cold weather
I'm off to me chateau in France!
Instead of jetting off to Gibraltar
Try a weekend in Scunthorpe with Walter.
I know they talk funny and it might not be sunny
But the language you won't have to alter.
At this time of year there's St Helens
Have you ever been there on your own?
As you walk down the street there's a spring in your feet
Knocks spots off visiting Rome.

144.

Google it when your boyfriends late.
You need to find an alternative date.
Google it when you've missed the train
And the taxi driver looks insane.
When modes of transport are unfit.....Google it.

Google it when you wonder why.
There's a funny rash on your inner thigh.
Or in that quiz you may be able
To Google your phone under the table.
When you friends you must outwit.....Google it.

Google it when you think you heard.
The mating call of a small brown bird.
Google it when you would have sweared.
But couldn't find the appropriate word.
Keeping quiet makes you a hypocrite.....Google it.

Google it when you need to find
The average size of a person's behind.
Say you're asking for a friend.
You'll feel less self conscious then.
So when those trousers just won't fit.........Google it.

Google it when your next door neighbour.
Sounds like he's going into labour.
God these party walls are thin.
He needs more tonic with his gin.
Can that noise come from a toilet sit ....Google it.

Google it when you're locked inside.
Chester Zoo on a Friday night.
You need to find a place to sleep.
With a pygmy goat or a blackface sheep.
Do you fancy one just a little bit......Google it.

Google it when your worlds gone wrong.
Or you need the words to an oblique song.
Google it when your world's gone mad.
And all you want is your mum and dad.
I promise I won't mention it......Google it.

145.

Melanie's Song.

You've broken your nails digging stones from your garden,
And your hair's soaking wet, pelted flat with the rain.
Your fine gentle hands are all cracked from cement,
And your worried about nothing again.
Don't bother with make up or designer clothes.
There's plenty of others dressed up in those.
When you're one of a kind,
You don't need to be,
Belonging to nothing but me.
You're finally sleeping after working all day.
With your unopened book by your silicone gun.
A half glass of wine left, a dog at your feet.
Plaster dust on your face in the sun.
Don't bother about being part of the in crowd.
You deserve some peace and all that's too loud.
When you're one of a kind,
You don't need to be,
Belonging to nothing but me.
I was so proud when we walked down the street.
With your mini-skirt wow and your blue snowstorm eyes.
We were just kids with the world at our feet.
Laughing free under bright summer skies.

146.

Look after the planet that created us.
Gave us water, food and comfort under the sunshine.
It never judged our faults and debated us.
Each day a perfect playground for our short time.
So now we burn its trees and stink its water.
Build skyscraper gaudy palaces, streets of cheap thrills.
Such a legacy for every son and daughter.
Planet silent, sunlight paints the dark hills.

147.

He glides round the strip in his Citroen Nemo.
Grey hair blowin' in the wind.
Blasting "Like a Rolling Stone" from his cassette deck.
Denim jacket really should be binned.
Sees an old granny in a mac.
Bent against the wind in pain.
Points her brolly at Chorley.
Shakes it and curses town and rain.
His life is like and old jumper.
Needs darning, sewing, elbow needs a patch.
Probably best to just unpick it.
And knit the bugger one more time from scratch.
He thinks most of the changes are mistaken.
He wonders where will this progress end.
Goes home for his egg and bacon.
Not me! Just asking for a friend.

148.

The Forget-me-nots I forgot
The sparkling birds that landed near us.
I didn't know their names or latin
Names, but they still feared us.
They saw us as the danger ones
When we felt overjoyed.
Like all god's innocent creatures
They know what to avoid.
Now the garden's overgrown
The weeds are green and fat.
They can have it back now.
You're gone and that is that.

149.

Plane flew low over the grey Mersey
Hovered then banged on the tarmac.
Smell the cool western air.
So many people in a hurry.
I waited in a bus shelter,
Looking at the streets and buildings.
Beatles wrote their masterpieces here.
Just another heart beating, another story.
Flat thin clouds, pink painting smear.
Rare moments of fleeting glory.

150.

I came in when the Teddy Boys were going out.
Spinning on the waltzer with a belly full of cider.
Beatles through black speakers blasting Twist and Shout.
A girl I couldn't talk to and another one beside her.
You can only sleep so much through boring school.
Eyes slowly closing, interest quickly lacking.
All the teachers knew I was a fool.
I was waiting for the future to get cracking.
We wandered lonely as four just men.
On the railway line to freedom and mortality.
Little did we know how short it was.
That gap between childhood and reality.

Epilogue.

The sun is sinking down over this northern town,
And I feel like I've been around this place forever.
But tomorrow I'll be gone, following that same sun.
There are some things though that distance cannot sever.
(chorus)
Fair blows the wind for France,
Fair blows the wind for Spain.
I'll be drinking wine in the warm sunshine
Instead of working in the rain.
With an old guitar in hand,
And somewhere warm to stand.
Fair blows the wind for France,
Fair blows the wind for Spain.

My Dad he died too soon, in a lifetime's afternoon,
So he never got the chance to see his evening.
But in our cages there are stars, if we just know where they are.
So I can celebrate his living without grieving.

The chimney's blowing smoke, and there's worn holes in my coat.
A letter from an old friend in my pocket.
With memories and ghosts and the things that matter most.
I can put them somewhere safe and never lock it.

Jim Berry copyright 2020.

Printed in Great Britain
by Amazon

28557864R10069